Alex Can't Sleep

A BEDTIME YOGA STORY

This book is for you!
Stay calm, keep breathing, and think positive. These are your superpowers—Cosmic Kids

PENGUIN YOUNG READERS LICENSES
An imprint of Penguin Random House LLC, New York

First published in the United States of America by Penguin Young Readers Licenses, an imprint of Penguin Random House LLC, New York, 2022

Visit us online at penguinrandomhouse.com.

Manufactured in China

ISBN 9780593386859   10 9 8 7 6 5 4 3 2 1 HH

Design by Taylor Abatiell

Alex Can't Sleep

A BEDTIME YOGA STORY

by Brooke Vitale
illustrated by Junissa Bianda

Alex lay in his bed, looking up at the stars on his ceiling. All the things that had happened that day ran through his mind, like a movie on repeat. He'd tried to block them out, but it was no use. They just kept playing.

Maybe a snack will help, he thought.

So, pushing back his covers, Alex **tiptoed** toward his door.

Alex made his way carefully down the dark hall. He'd walked this hall thousands of times, but in the dark, it felt different. He gently ran his fingers along the wall, moving slowly so he wouldn't trip and wake anyone.

Suddenly . . . "Ouch!" Alex whispered. His foot had landed on something hard and pointy.

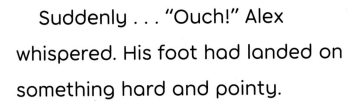

Bending over, he picked up the thing he'd stepped on.

Alex looked at the thing in his hand. It was a chewed-up dog bone. "Ugh, Spence," he said.

Hearing his name, the **dog** came running. He pushed his wet nose against Alex's hand and started to whimper.

"Okay, okay," Alex said, rubbing Spence's head.
"I'll get you a snack, too."

Together, Spence and Alex walked to the kitchen.

"Let's see," he said, swinging open the refrigerator **door**.

"Ooh! Cake!"

But as Alex reached into the refrigerator, the kitchen light came on.

Spinning around, Alex found
Mom standing in the doorway.

"Can't sleep, huh?" she said,
smiling.

Alex **shook** his head.

"How about a glass of warm
milk?" she asked.

Now it was Alex's turn to smile. That sounded good to him.

Alex sat by the kitchen table as Mom poured out the milk. He hoped this would make him sleepy.

Alex wiped the milk mustache from his face and followed Mom back to his room.

Throwing himself down on his bed, he let out a few big sighs.

"Hey, bud," Mom said, patting his head. "What's wrong? Is something bothering you?"

Alex sighed again and shook his head. Kicking his legs up on the **wall**, he looked up at Mom. He laughed a little. She looked upside down now!

Finally, he said, "Today was bad. My favorite chair was taken in class. My toy broke during playtime. And at lunch, I dropped my sandwich in the dirt."

"I'm sorry today was so tough," Mom said. "But tomorrow will be better."

Alex heaved himself around to face Mom and **hugged his knees**.

"How do you know?" he asked. "What if tomorrow I drop my sandwich *and* my apple? What if there are no red crayons? What if . . ."

Alex trailed off, too upset to think about the next what-if.

Mom smiled and reached over to give Alex a **hug**. "It's called hope," she said. "We don't know if tomorrow will be better, worse, or the same. But we can always hope it will be better. That's how we push on."

"You know," Mom said, rubbing Alex's back, "when I've had a hard day, I find it helps to take deep, centering breaths."

"Deep, centering breaths?" Alex asked, confused.

"What does that mean?"

"I'll show you," Mom said.

Crossing her legs, she put her palms on her knees and closed her eyes. "A centered breath means you focus on your breath. **Breathe out** all the bad of today and **breathe in** the good you hope will come tomorrow."

Alex watched Mom for a minute. Then he tried to do what she was doing.

"Hey, that does feel better!" he said.

Mom smiled. "How about a song?" she said.

Alex nodded. "I'd like that."

Unwinding his legs, he lay down with his head on Mom's lap and listened to her sing.

When Mom was done, Alex snuggled up under his covers.
Brushing his hair aside, Mom clicked off his lamp and gave him a kiss
on the forehead. Then she started for his door.

"Mom?" Alex asked nervously. "What if I still can't sleep?"

"Then you try breathing again," Mom said. "Come on. Let's take a few deep breaths together. As you breathe in, count to four in your head. As you breathe out, count to six."

Alex tried Mom's counting. Slowly, his eyes started to close as he **relaxed**. His arms fell to the sides, and his breath became even.

In no time, he was fast asleep.

COSMIC KIDS!

Try these **relaxing poses** to fall asleep like Alex!

Tiptoe Pose

Forward Bend Pose

Legs Up the Wall Pose

Neck Turns Pose

Door Pose

Dog Pose

Knee Hugging Pose

Hugs Pose

Mouse Pose

Easy Pose

Relaxation Pose

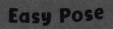